I0589751

ry dog

pet in

2016

every dog i pet in 2016

copyright © 2017 joseph parker okay

cover art by moss angel
book design by joseph parker okay

the scanning, uploading, and distribution of this book via the internet or any other means is fine. if you steal this book that's fine. really you should steal more things. steal from grocery stores if you can. definitely never pay for movies. buy music if you're able to, unless the artist is on the radio or a major label. if you can't afford it tho that's fine steal music too.

isbn-10: 0-9994723-1-3
isbn-13: 978-0-9994723-1-6

maudlinhouse.net
@maudlinhouse

every breed of dog on earth is descendent from grey wolves, and that seems impossible, but most things i don't understand seem impossible so this is probably fine

1.1 ~ ~ third quarter

skylar! this is my mom's gray and black 4 year old aussie doodle and wow i'm so excited she's the first dog i'm petting this year. i didn't go out last night but instead just lied in bed and finished the second draft of a short story about a person with a drinking problem who gets ghosted by the void (later in the year an updated version of this story appeared in witch craft magazine and then even later was included in my first book). today was the first time i started a new year by not being violently hungover since i was like 17. i had the day off and nothing to do so i drove ~30 minutes to my mom's house—which is the same house i grew up in and also the same house my mom and her 6 siblings grew up in—to see her and my sister siera. skylar always greets me outside by running back and forth between jumping up on the side fence and jumping up on the side of the house. my mom's stopped cleaning it bc it just gets dirty again right away, so there's all these black and muddy-like paw prints along the side of the blue house paneling. mom was getting a pile of things together to take to goodwill and asked if i wanted anything from it before it all got donated. i picked up an old electric typewriter and moved it over by the door so i'd remember to take it when i left.

mom unfolded a blanket made out of a fabric with horses printed on it and said the daughter of one of my dad's old coworkers had made it for my dad when he first started chemo. she handed it to me and i stared at it and just kept saying, "this is really good."

1.25 ~ ~ full

it's like 10 am and i'm walking out the door of my apartment building while my landlord is walking in and i say "how's it going" and he says "cold" and i say "yes." i'm already running late for work and as i look up the street trying to remember where i parked last night, i see a woman who i've met a few times while drinking on the front stoop with jake late at night. sometimes she comes out to take her small brown pup to use the bathroom and jake and i say hi to her and talk in baby talk to the dog on their way out and back in. i don't remember either of their names now but i say hi in a way i think is probably too friendly for the few times we've met. her dog is wearing a small blue sweater and playing in the snow and this will probably be the only time i genuinely smile all day.

1.30 ~ ~ waning gibbous

rarely are there breaks in the milwaukee winter and it's even more rare when they happen on one of my days off. it was almost 30 degrees out so i went for a walk along lake michigan and ended up going all the way out to the end of the harbor's break wall and back. this part of the lakefront holds so many memories for me; i've been coming here since i was in high school to watch the waves and i've brought every major love interest i've ever had to this exact place. i only saw one dog today and it's v surprising (read: disappointing) more people weren't out with their pets in this weather. this dog was medium sized and white with brownish-red marks and ears. it was running ahead of its owners and then running back to them, they were walking slower than me and i ended up passing them. the dog ran past me and then on its way back it stopped right in front of me. after i scratched its head a little it jumped back and did i little stutter step then ran out in front of me again and then back to its owners.

2.14 ~ ~ first quarter

i walked with marissa and her roommate the few blocks from their house in riverwest to bremen's cafe. when we got there we could hear a band in the back covering pedro the lion songs. it was an event marissa's friend was putting on and marissa seemed to know the majority of the people there. i rarely go out and even though marissa introduced me to most of the people she talked to i still felt uncomfortable. we watched the band for a little bit and then got more drinks. jake was sitting at the bar and he bought the three of us a round of tequila shots. i went back in the room where the music was playing and a my chemical romance cover band was setting up. i didn't know where marissa was and i was starting to feel extremely anxious and upset with myself. i'd really been looking forward to going out tonight and being social again but i think i've spent an irreversible amount of time alone and instead of enjoying being out i just wanted to cry and be teleported back home so i could pet my cat and listen to beach house in bed. i took a sip from my beer and still felt exactly the same. i didn't know where to look so i looked down at my feet and instead of seeing my feet i saw a large black dog with brown markings looking up at me. i pet the dog and asked if it was having a good time. it wondered off and shortly after that marissa found me in the crowd and then jake found us and we all danced and sang along to songs i hadn't heard in years.

2.20 ~ ~ waxing gibbous

my sister angela invited me over to her and her husband's house for dinner so we could see each other before i move to tucson. she texted me and asked what i wanted to eat and i said tacos would be good and she said, "can tacos be vegan?"

"yea, it's just like regular tacos. without meat and cheese."

dinner was weird bc my sister just talked nonstop shit about other people in our family and i couldn't help thinking this is probably the same way she talks about me when i'm not around. at one point she said she didn't think it was a good idea for me to move to arizona bc she "doesn't want to get another phone call." this was in reference to when i'd lived in arizona 4 years ago and had my first panic attack and didn't know how to handle it. i called my mom crying and told her a lot of scary-sounding things including how i couldn't "picture myself in the future".

"i didn't call you, i called mom."

"who do you think mom called afterwards?"

i know she's probably not aware of it, but no matter what angela talks about she always finds a way to make it about herself. it really hurt that she was basically saying that my poor mental health is a burden to her, and she wanted me to keep being miserable in wisconsin just so it would reduce the possibility of the chemical imbalances in my brain of effecting her in the future.

after dinner we continued sitting around the table talking and her husband's dog marley* came up to me and put his head on my lap. marley is a big and old white lab with an enlarged heart that makes it difficult to drink water and keep food down. angela calls him 'the polar bear' and i usually refer to him as 'marles barkley'. marley coughed up some phlegmy stuff on my leg and angela's husband said, "did he just throw up on you?" i said "oh no it's fine" as i reached for a pile of napkins.

---

* r.i.p. marley

3.1 ~ ~ third quarter

jake and i started driving to tucson yesterday. he's in his car with some of my stuff and i'm in mine with the rest of it. we just crossed the border into northern texas and it's a true wasteland. my fuel light's been on for awhile but all the gas stations we pass are abandoned and look like they have been for awhile. we finally get to a real gas station after almost an hour and a half and it's busier than i expected it to be. the card reader at the pump is broken and when i go inside to pay the cashier says "welcome to nowhere." i set the nozzle on "autopilot" and sit in my car with the door open and my legs hanging out of it. i'm scrolling through twitter and all of a sudden there are 2 greyhound-like dogs in front of me. they look almost identical except one has a heavy green cast on its right front leg. a man standing near the open door of a pickup truck on the other side of the parking lot whistles and the dogs run towards him and jump into the truck. the man waves and then drives away.

3.2 ~ ~ **third quarter**

tucson! i can't believe we frickin made it. ok i guess i'm not surprised we made it i'm just surprised i'm here at all. we pulled up in front of boost house and jackson was sitting on the porch smoking. we hugged and they led us inside where we were immediately greeted by a barking charlie dog—a small chihuahua mix that belongs to e.e., another one of my new roommates. charlie calmed down after not that long but still barked each time jake or i came into the house carrying stuff from the cars to my new room.

3.4 ~ ~ waning crescent

boost house is screening a documentary in a few days so i drove e.e. and jackson over to their friends' place to pick up a projector and there were 3 medium-big sized dogs there. one was dark brown, another was light brown with dark brown markings, and the other was white with light brown markings and was wearing a camo bandana. the first 2 were pit mixes maybe? tbh who cares they were cute as heck.

3.6 ~ ~ waning crescent

alexandr and ray and i drove to savers and i was excited bc they also live at boost house and this is the first real chance i've had to hang out with them. when we pulled into the parking lot we saw an old man walking the tiniest cream-colored pupper. i said "omg that's the smallest dog i've ever seen in my entire life" and ray told me not to let e.e. hear me say things like that about any dog that isn't charlie. she said e.e. is "very protective" about charlie's size. a few minutes later i was looking around an aisle full of weird bowls and glasses and when i walked out of the aisle there was the tiny dog staring up at me. it's owner had his back to me and was looking at something on a shelf so i did a sneaky pet and blew it a kiss and then walked away.

3.8 ~ ~ new

tonight is my first tinder date in tucson. we meet at a dog-friendly bar. sara buys the first round of drinks, and while we're at the bar ordering it seems like she's friends with most of the people behind the counter. we find an open table and sit down and talk about what she's going to school for and why i moved to tucson. while we're talking a small-medium prince charles puppy walks up to our table and stares up at us. we both pet him enthusiastically and the person on the other end of his leash talks to us for a little bit. the pup's name is finigan and holy shit this dog had these round, bulging eyes and i want to cry just remembering them.

i got the next round and after that she invited me back to her place. when we got there we were met at the door by 2 barking doggos. one was hers, a dark brown/reddish wiener dog mix who really doesn't like guys. kelsey said he was a rescue pup and used to have a very abusive owner. she said charlie is really productive of her and once bit her ex in the butt while they were fricking. the other dog was her roommate's lemon beagle named sashi who is one of the most sweetest dogs i've ever met. sara said one of her other roommates had 2 big doberman pinchers but that roomy had left for awhile and had taken the dogs with her.

3.11 ~ ~ waxing crescent

tucson is really weird, you can drive 20 minutes out of the city and it feels like you're in the middle of nowhere. sara picked me up early this morning so we could go to the desert museum before it got too hot out. it's a mostly outdoor exhibit of animals and bugs and rocks and garden that feels like its in the middle of nowhere. they have multiple aviaries and one that's exclusively filled with hummingbirds that are indifferent about humans and will fly up right next to you. while walking along one of the outdoor trails we saw rustling in the tall grass and out popped a small squirrel. i put my hand out to it and it must be used to humans feeding it bc it came close enough for me to rub its little head. i said "thank you friend" and then it turned around and hopped back into the grass.

we walked around the entire museum and it wasn't even noon by the time we left. sara said she wanted to take me somewhere really special and that it was a surprise. we drove to the other side of town and when we got close she made me close my eyes. she parked too close to the tall building for me to read the sign on it and when we got inside someone told us they had to hold onto our drivers license while we were there.

we walked into another room and!!! there were dogs!!!! 9 dogs in 5 different crates and they all looked like different breeds of puppies. we got to hold and play with each one and then we went to the back of the room and there were 2 kittens that we played with too.

when we got back into sara's car i said "wow this is the greatest date i've been on in my entire life."

3.17 ~ ~ waxing gibbous

zuul is a 7 month old pug who's owner is staying at boost house for a few days. he's basically the naughtiest dog in the world but so adorable he gets away with everything. this dog could literally murder me and i'd still love him.

3.19 ~ ~ waxing gibbous

today i went for a hike up mount lemmon with alexandr, e.e., jackson, julie, and charlie dog. when we got to the top we sat and had a picnic and while we were snacking some other people came up who had an absolutely beautiful dog named cody. he looked like a cross between an australian shepherd and a wolf. charlie and cody started kind of fighting and it was scary. i was the closest to the dogs so i tried to push them apart and ended up just picking charlie up and taking her over to e.e.. the people talked to us for a little bit about the beautiful view and then they kept walking. e.e. wrapped charlie up in a blanket in their lap and she seemed to calm down pretty quick.

3.31 ~ ~ third quarter

luna and ryder!! sara's roommate is back home and these are her 2 doberman pinchers. they both big and intimidating but so gentle. ryder is brown and always wears a bandana and luna is gray and completely deaf.

4.12 ~ ~ first quarter

4 dogs today!! sara and i drove to tempe for a mutual friend's gallery opening. we got to the city early so we went to a bar on mill ave for dinner and drinks. we sat on the patio and while we were waiting for our food a man walked up with 2 doggos and sat at the bar. his medium-small black dog jumped up on the stool next to him but the small fluffy white dog stayed on the ground and looked up like he was jealous the other dog could jump up that high. i went to the bathroom and on my way back to our table i stopped and pet the dogs and talked to the guy for a little bit. he told me he was a veteran and that now he makes his own jewelry out of things like scrap metal and bullet casings.

after we got done eating sara and i walked down mill towards asu. when we got to the gallery i ran into some people i hadn't seen since i lived in tempe 4 years ago. we didn't really keep in touch so it was mostly just awkward. there was a snack table that was just fortune cookies and poptarts on a fancy platter. we made friends with someone who was holding a small and sort-of-worried looking wiener dog.

when we left it was dark out and we decided to

grab another drink and walk around beach park. while walking back down mill we passed a very large husky lying on a bar patio that looked really tired. when i pet it its eyes opened but it didn't move its head to see who was touching it. after drinks and the lake we got doughnuts at a shop called 'the fractured prune' and then drove back home.

4.20 ~ ~ full

i sat in front of my computer in the living room with e.e. and steve watching a poetry reading that luis neer had set up on tinychat. shy watson read, then carmen brady. after carmen read e.e. and i walked to a house show at their friends' place. i didn't know anyone there so i started drinking beer bc i didn't know what else to do with my hands and mouth. i talked to someone carrying a 6 month old black lab named byron who kept falling asleep and then half waking up. i talked to someone else who asked what i did and i told him i ran a literary journal called spy kids review and he seemed really confused by the name and asked if it was a magazine for children. after the show ended ~8 of us started dancing wildly to songs someone was playing thru the speakers. the only ones i remember now are the ymca, all star, party in the usa, and something by the spice girls.

5.14 ~ ~ waxing gibbous

today was the day i finally met wulfie!! ok so this is julie's dog who i've been hearing about ever since i moved here and somehow haven't met until now, at julie's graduation party. he's an extremely cute brown pit bull and way larger than i thought he'd be. his nickname is megatron and he's definitely earned it. i brought watermelon infused beer and it turned into a dance party. a lot of us went up on the roof and sat really close to each other. i tried taking a selfie with the moon but there wasn't enough light.

6.2 ~ ~ **waning crescent**

tonight i did my first reading ever and then directly afterwards put sunglasses on charlie*.

6.20 ~ ~ full (summer solstice)

i went to a park with e.e. and charlie to watch the sunset. hp and tom, artists from london who have been living at boost house this month, came too. for the past few days there's been a lot of rain and wind and this small park looked almost post-apocalypitc with fallen trees and debris scattered all over. it was raining lightly and the way the sun was setting amongst the storm clouds made it look like the world was truly ending. we sat on a bench next to a fallen tree and watched charlie do her dog thing. another dog came up and started trying to play with charlie, but she didn't seem to be in that friendly of a mood and started barking. the dog was tan-ish and almost medium sized and looked part deer. the dog's owner came jogging up and said "sorry, jax is just looking for a friend" and then led him away. a little later someone else showed up with 2 large fancy-looking poodles, one red and one gray. we all went over to talk to the owner and play with the dogs, who ended up being named chili and liger. another person showed up with almost identical looking small white and brown dogs who were sisters named solé and luna. charlie was suddenly in a much friendlier mood and jax showed up again and all 6 doggos played together for what seemed like a really long time until it got too dark out and we all had to go.

32

6.21 ~ ~ full

i don't remember what time it was exactly but it was early, like before 8am, and i was just getting home from a run. when i was a block away i could see the shape of a big black dog walking up the sidewalk toward me and then stopping to sniff around our front yard. by the time i got up there he was sniffing the mailbox. he was friendly and when i started petting and talking to him he mostly just ignored me and continued sniffing around the mailbox. he trotted away and i went inside and went back to bed. when i woke up again i realized i should have checked if the dog had a collar bc he definitely seemed lost and i could have helped get him back home. i'm not sure why it didn't cross my mind to do that in the moment. i still think about this pupper sometimes and i hope he's safe.

7.3 ~ ~ new

the lease at boost house ended a few days ago. alexandr and ray got their own place closer to downtown and steve and i found an apartment on the northside. besides us 4 everyone else moved out of az. steve left for tour a little over a week ago before we were scheduled to move into our new place so i ended up moving both of our stuff by myself, which wasn't too bad bc we both don't own that much but time consuming bc i could only move it in my small compact car. i did rent a uhaul for the bigger stuff that sara helped me with. she'd gotten back together with her ex or soemthing and this was the last time we saw each other.

okok sry enough of the context setting lets get back to the dogs. oh wait this one needs more back story so just hold in there a little longer. my friend shannon from tempe had a few days off work and wanted a change of scenery and asked if she could come crash on my couch for the weekend. we only knew each other from twitter before this and had been pen pals for a short time when i lived in milwaukee. today's the last day of her visit and we drove to a rose garden to watch the sunset and right outside of it was a grove of olive trees with cicada husks all over them. we were looking at the husks when an older lady* walking a large white and light brown spotted dog came up to us and asked what we were doing. shannon told her while i started petting her dog and then the old lady asked us if we were entomologists.

---

* shannon and i are roommates in tucson now and shannon ran into this same woman at a green party meeting in june 2017. she didn't remember shannon.

7.4 ~ ~ **new**

my friend laura from twitter invited me to go to a party in tempe with her roommate maya (who i only knew from twitter too) and some of their friends. i drove up and sat in their living room with laura and her dog maisey and their friend drew while we waited for maya and lexi to get ready. maisey is a chubby yellow doxen/corgi mix. we played fetch down a hallway for a little bit and then drew drove us all to the party. i didn't want to drink but felt awkward so i did. a couple hours into the party someone showed up carrying a small pomeranian puppy named ava. it ended up being a really big party. laura got a phone call and then said she had to go. i thought drew had been drinking but it turned out he was sober. i was really impressed that he could be at a party and not drink and i decided i wanted to try doing that at parties in the future bc i want to feel the same way about myself that i felt about drew.

we ghosted out of the party and drew drove the 4 of us to a gas station where i bought an energy drink and a gallon of water. we went to a much smaller party at a house called "the swamp". in the back there was a big in-ground pool and 2 dogs. one of the dogs was a small/medium sized brown pitbull named tom that kept jumping in the pool and the other was a 3 legged medium sized white pit bull who kept chasing a ball me and maya and drew took turns throwing.

the next day i started following lexi on twitter and it turns out she has literally the cutest little puppy in the world and my heart breaks into a million pieces every time she tweets a photo of her.

7.7 ~ ~ waxing crescent

julie invited me to a dance party at someone's house. i biked there and felt really awkward. julie had invited me in a "come socialize with other people" way and not in a "come hangout with me" way, the difference between the 2 being she knew just about everyone there, so she couldn't just hang out with me the whole time, she had to split up her time between people and groups. julie's moving to austin soon for grad school and she's been trying to get all the ppl she's friends with to be friends with each other, but this was the first social function after i decided to try being sober in uncomfortable social settings, and on top of how awkward that made me feel i was also really sweaty from the bike ride. i sat outside alone and played pokemon go on my phone. someone showed up to the party with an almost-puppy black pit bull wearing a blue harness. this was one of the chillest dogs i've ever seen it just walked up to me and wagged its tail for a little bit and then moved on to other ppl. there was a low-ish wall some people were climbing up and then jumping from it onto the roof. after a little bit i was just like "ok fuck it" and got onto the roof too. it was flat up there and surprisingly big. there were 3 other people all drinking beer and i joined in their conversation and actually had a good time. i walked over to the other side of the roof and peed off it while looking out at grant road, which is usually pretty busy but was completely dead at that moment.

7.10 ~ ~ first quarter

bonecow!! ok so this needs some backstory; bonecow is ray's mostly-white dog that has black markings and a mostly black head/face. he was in new england with ray's family the whole time we lived together but, after boost house ended, ray went back home to visit and she brought cow with her when she returned to tucson. i've heard so much about this pup i'm so glad he's here in the desert and we get to be friends.

7.15 ~ ~ waxing gibbous

skylar!!! okay this is my mom's dog again but i'm visiting for the first time in ~4 months and i've missed this pupper so much. i flew into chicago yesterday for the thesis gallery reception of jake's mfa program and spent the night at his dorm. this morning my sister siera picked me up and drove me back to milwaukee to stay with her and my mom for a couple days.

7.17 ~ ~ waxing gibbous

i'm back in chicago today, siera dropped me off early this morning. jake and i went for a walk around the city and found a mediterranean place to eat. on our way back to his dorm we stopped to pet a small and fluffy white dog with light brown markings tied to a locked bike outside of some tourist-y apparel store.

7.18 ~ ~ full

today's my last day in the midwest, i fly back to arizona at 10pm tonight. it took a long time but i convinced jake to wake up early this morning and walk down to the lakefront to watch the sunrise over lake michigan. i used to do this all the time by myself when we lived together in milwaukee but i needed him to come with me otherwise i couldn't get past the security checkpoint and back into the dorms. on our way back we stopped at walgreens on state and roosevelt to get some food. when we walked out we had to wait to cross the street and standing in front of us was a medium sized white and dark brown pit bull. its owner had his back turned to us and i pet the side of the pup's happy face and it licked my hand all over. after we crossed the street jake said "sneaky dog friend."

7.23 ~ ~ waning gibbous

today i tried right swiping a picture of a dog on instagram.

7.30 ~ ~ waning crescent

i'm back in tucson now and on a tinder date with jordan. we're walking to a park near her house to watch the sunset and we go by 2 ppl with a medium size brown dog. the people pass by first and then i bend down and let my hand drag over the dog's back and whisper "good, good." jordan, who was walking behind me, started to laugh and loudly said, "did you just pet that dog?"

8.1 ~ ~ new

a man walking a fluffy husky in a grocery store parking lot mistook scout for someone he knew and then said "sorry I thought you were someone I know." I said "that's okay, you have a beautiful dog" and he said thanks and told us its name. we walked a little further and the dog walked kind of near me and I awkwardly pet it and I think it creeped out the guy bc he stopped and pulled his dog away and stood there until scout and I were inside the store.

8.4 ~ ~ waxing crescent

steve ordered a lyft for him, scout, and me to the greyhound station so we could catch a bus to the phoenix airport. the bus ended up being really late and we got off it before our last stop because the bus driver was being an idiot and said he was going to take a 20 minute break there for basically no real reason. at this point we were super stressed out bc it was getting too close to our take off time and we thought for sure we weren't going to make it. steve got us another lyft and while we were waiting for it to show up the bus left and it felt bad bc i wasn't sure if we'd made the right choice, but once we got on the highway we ended up passing the bus and that felt really good. we only had carry ons so once we got to the airport we all sprinted to the other end where the security check was. they searched both steve's and scout's bags by slowly taking each item out and leaving them in a big mess on the table and then steve and scout had to repack them. we sprinted again from there to our gate and even tho we were late the ppl working at the gate were really nice and said the plane had waited a little longer for us to show up.

we got to denver and holy crap i forgot how huge this airport is. scout and steve were talking a lot about how it's the "most satanic" airport and we spent some time walking around and looking at the paintings in it. it truly did seem like a satanic place. we took an escalator underground to catch the train to take us to the other side of the airport and a few ppl ahead of us was a man carrying a medium-large golden retriever who was looking back at us. i really wanted to pet the dog so i could write about it in this journal and talk about how crazy this day has been, but once we got to the ground floor it was packed with people and i lost track of where the man and the dog went. a train showed up and a lot of people got on and the three of us were up next to get on but it was already really full so we decided to wait for the next one. while we waited i saw someone else with a dog but it was wearing an emotional support harness and i wasn't sure if those have the same rules as service dogs, like you're not supposed to pet or ask to pet them, so i didn't. when the next train got there people seemed to rush onto it all at once and in the commotion i felt something weird brush against my leg. when i looked down i saw the emotional support dog standing there and my first thought was, "this counts."

8.6 ~ ~ waxing crescent

tonight was the second night of 'this lil lit fest', a 3-day event for small publishers in denver put together by catch business. spy kids review's showcase reading happened tonight at a nice bar/small theater. catch, scout, and steve all read with me talking in between and introducing them. a lot more people showed up for it than i thought were going to. afterward catch had an open mic style reading in their backyard and a lot of ppl showed up for that too. someone brought a medium-big white lab and i don't remember what his name was but it was something wacky and adorable like booper. i was in the living room with a few other people when the dog walked in by itself and i said i was really happy it was there bc 1) i love dogs and 2) it meant i could write about tonight in this journal. someone asked to hear what i have so far so i took out my phone and read very condensed versions from the beginning up until zuul and stopped there bc i thought that was the funniest entry so far and i wanted to end it on a high note.

8.7 ~ ~ waxing crescent

tonight was the last night of this lil lit fest. it ended with another publishing house's reading at an indie book store. partway through the reading scout and steve left bc scout's mom's boyfriend works for an artist-management company and had gotten them free tickets to a slipknot concert. after the reading we were all outside talking and i looked up and saw a woman crossing the street walking the cutest tiny dachshund. i tried pointing it out to the people around me without physically pointing bc i didn't want the woman to feel weirded out that we were all looking in her direction but once she got close enough i asked if i could pet her dog, which is something i rarely feel comfortable enough to do, but she was enthusiastic when she said yes and there were like 5 or 6 of us all squatted down to pet him. she talked to us for a couple minutes about the dog and i felt engaged in the conversation but now i think i was just on social-autopilot mode bc i can't remember anything except the dog. shortly after the woman left we all left too. i drove catch's suv back to her house bc i was the only sober person in our group. while we were driving jackson rolled down a window and yelled something about god loving weed to a car full of high schoolers. we stopped at a grocery store and ended up seeing those same high schoolers in the store. jackson was really high and kept saying they should go apologize for yelling at the kids but then just continued standing still.

8.18 ~ ~ full

alexandr and i were having a "work party", which is basically when we hangout in the same place but work on our own things on our computers. we decided we needed coffee before we started so we went to the coffee shop where they work. while we were there a man w a brown dog that looked like a younger and more muscular version of scooby doo came in and sat in the back. at one point the man got up to get a cup of water and the dog started giving little barks and prancing around like it was afraid he was going to leave and it was extremely cute and endearing. on our way out we walked past them and i bent down to pet the pup and it bit me gently and held my hand in its mouth as if to say "please be nice, i only want nice people petting me." i gave him a small chin scratch and then left.

9.2 ~ ~ new

i had a dream i was petting 3 dogs and woke up really disappointed that it was only a dream. (this happened to me a few times throughout the year but this is the only time i wrote it down.)

9.9 ~ ~ first quarter

2 days ago i went out for pho with jonathan and then went to a show he organized but wasn't playing. he told me he was renting a beach house in newport beach for 3 weeks with a bunch of his friends and asked if i wanted to come with. i didn't know if he was serious or not but i said, "hell yeah." the next day we didn't talk at all so i figured he wasn't actually being serious about the invitation but then this morning i woke up to a text from him asking what time i could be ready. he picked me up and said we were going to spend a couple of days in las vegas visiting his family and drive to newport from there.

shortly after crossing the az/nv border jonathan said, "we just went over the hoover dam" and i said, "i didn't even know that was on this side of the country."

we got to jonathan's sister's house and a small gray poodle named maggie came out to greet us and barked a little. jonathan told me maggie is 15 and then said "she's defying death so hard right now." we went into the house and there was a small black and brown dog named booty standing on a very large pillow and barking at us. i didn't try to pet him bc he seemed so freaked out. we walked passed a closed door and his sister said "there's another psycho dog in there i'm not even going to try bringing out" and i felt sad and softly patted the door as i walked by it.

9.10 ~ ~ first quarter

we took jonathan's car to an auto place so he could get the tires changed. while we waited for it to be done we walked around vegas. i took pictures of the clouds and stores i thought had wacky names. when we went back to pick up the car there was an old lady sharing her seat with a v small fluffy gray dog. the woman looked scared about being out in public and i felt bad about approaching her to ask if i could pet the dog so i just made eye contact with it and did a little head nod.

9.11 ~ ~ waxing gibbous

this morning we woke up at 6 and started driving. the first thing we did when we got to newport was stop at the grocery store. it was my first time in a trader joe's. we drove to the beach house and the cleaning service was still there picking up after the last guests, so we drove like an extra block and parked along the beach. we went to a little shop and bought flip flops and sun block. we sat down outside to put the flips flops on and someone with an australian shepherd came up to us. they talked to us mostly about our tattoos and i wasn't really paying attention to the conversation bc i was too busy petting the dog.

i forgot flip flops suck to walk in so i carried them and walked barefoot in the sand next to the boardwalk. we walked a long way and the bottom of my feet hurt and i thought it was just bc the sand was hot, but then there was a sharp stabbing pain under one of my toes. i thought i'd stepped on a seashell or something but when i looked at the bottom of my foot there was a large, broken-open blister that was completely filled with sand. i got back on the boardwalk and put on my flip flops and walked back to the car as carefully as i could. when we got there i sat down on the curb and washed my foot with water and found there was a blister in the exact same place on my other foot that hadn't burst open yet. we drove back to the house and the cleaning people were gone. i washed my foot off better and put a bandaid over both the blisters.

later we walked back to the beach to swim and watch the sunset. there weren't that many people there and it bummed me out bc either 1) people here don't care about the sunset, or 2) there's a way better place to watch the sunset that we don't know about. the sunset was great tho and this was my first time ever swimming in the ocean. jonathan and i did handstands in the sand until it got too cold for us to be outside and wet.

9.13 ~ ~ waxing gibbous

a bunch of jonathan's friends showed up sunday night and yesterday. i've met 3 of them before but there are ~7 other people who i don't know at all. this morning most of us walked to get coffee at a place that was right on the beach. on our way there i told everyone i had a goal of petting 5 dogs today. it was overcast but the air still felt nice. outside the coffeehouse were 2 old women sitting on a tall planter who had a very large great dane named duchess. i talked with them for a little while and then went inside to join everyone else again.

after we got coffee we walked up a really tall pier that was nearby and i saw a sea lion for the first time. i heard a group of them barking somewhere and someone told me it was bc the locals were throwing them fish.

today is sam's birthday and her and kelsea and alex all want to go out for drinks and i offered to be their dd. i like being dd bc i like knowing my friends are safe. i drove kelsea's car to a bar she had heard about that ended up being on the top floor of an outside mall. we parked and while walking to it we passed by someone walking a medium/large golden retriever. the owner passed by us first and said hi and as the dog passed i did a sneaky pet. the bar turned out be literally the fanciest bar any of us had ever been to. the balcony overlooked the ocean and as we stepped out onto it 'all along the watchtower' by jimi hendrix began to play.

9.14 ~ ~ waxing gibbous

jonathan is staying in newport until the end of the month but i'm starting a new job in a few days so i caught a ride back to az with 2 of his friends who had driven here together. the window i sat next to in the backseat was warped in a way that added a rainbow overlay to everything i looked out at. we took a detour thru los angeles where the people driving used to live so they could meet up with one of their friends. we met him at a ramen place that didn't have any good vegan options so i didn't end up getting anything. when their friend showed up he talked a lot about some of the music videos the company he worked for had shot recently. he said they had a big client recently and showed us a picture on his phone of drake standing next to some cameras and an expensive looking car. at one point someone walked in with a black lab and tied it to the table. when we got up to leave the dog's owner had gone to the bathroom so i pet the dog and it lifted its head a little and then put it back down.

9.18 ~ ~ waning gibbous

steve and i were biking home from the gym and when we got to our apartment complex a medium yellow lab/pit bull mix (maybe, not completely sure) without a collar ran out of the parking area and around the corner. i put my bike against a wall and followed it around to a long gate with vertical bars. there was a black lab behind the gate. i bent down and pet the yellow dog. it was skittish at first and seemed afraid of my hands but it warmed up to me v quick. the black dog started to whimper a little so i walked over to the gate and pet it and it was really friendly. the yellow dog followed me over to my bike and then turned around and walked over by the gate again. i put my bike inside the apartment and went back out. the yellow dog was trying to get itself thru the gate but it kept getting stuck. when it saw me walking up it ran over by me and started doing little jumps. the black dog started barking and whimpering again and the yellow dog went over by it. i went and walked around my apartment complex trying to find someone who was looking for a dog but had no luck. a car slowly drove past me and stopped and i asked if they were looking for a dog but i think they misheard me bc all they said was "good luck." when i walked back over by the gate the yellow dog was on the other side of it and playing with the black dog. i pet them both thru the gate and then went back home.

10.5 ~ ~ waxing crescent

a couple weeks ago i started working at a call center for verizon wireless and i made friends with a lot of the people in my training class. one of those people was emily and after she found out i'm vegan she insisted she set me up with one of her best friends, krista, who's also vegan. i dm'd krista on instagram and we talked for awhile and made plans to go on a ~6 hour hike as a 'first date'. when i got to her house she walked outside carrying a tiny and super skinny rescue pup she had adopted ~5 days before. we walked in her house and 2 small adult dogs started barking. one was a lil wiener dog named rigby and the other some kind of chihuahua mix named mordecai.

after the hike we were exhausted and sweaty and she asked if i wanted to go hang out with her friends and i was like, "okay." we went over to her friend brandon's place and he had a small and energetic dog that i kept referring to as "pristine". krista told me brandon named the dog toulouse bc he's obsessed with ariana grande and ariana grande has a dog named toulouse.

10.6 ~ ~ first quarter

mom came to az so she could visit me in tucson and then my aunt and uncle in prescott valley. she flew into phoenix and drove to my apartment. i introduced her to steve and picked up my cat mil and said "look grandma's here." we got into her rental car and went to the hotel she was staying at. i helped her bring her bags up to her room and then we drove back to my apartment complex and got into my car. i wanted to drive so she could enjoy looking at the surroundings as we drove through tucson. i took her to my favorite restaurant for a burrito and then we went hiking at gates pass. i took a selfie with mom's iphone and then she asked me to send it to siera and angela. i drove us back to her rental car and then we drove separately back to her hotel. we sat around the pool talking for a long time. i felt bad because i was tired from the long day before and at times couldn't think of anything to say. we sat in silence for awhile but it felt nice to be occupying the same space as her after so long of not seeing her. when it started to get dark we went inside and turned on the tv and space jam was on. we watched it for awhile and she talked about how we used to watch this movie together a lot when i was a little kid. i cried a little in the elevator as i was leaving and when i stepped out of it i almost walked into a guy who had two kids with him as well as a standard looking family-type yellow lab. the dad was carrying what looked like everyone's bags as well as holding onto the leash. the dog looked so stressed and i felt bad and didn't want to stress it out more by trying to pet it so i just waved at it as i walked by.

10.13 ~ ~ waxing gibbous

emily started dating our supervisor julia. it was a big secret and for some reason i'm the only one she told about it. the other day while i was sitting at a table full of other people from our class in the lunch room, emily walked in and whispered "i just fingered julia in the bathroom" in my ear. emily and i walked back to the classroom and while we were talking she rubbed her hands together and smelled them and said "i should have washed my hands."

"wait you didn't wash your hands after you fingered her?"

"it's not like she's gross down there."

we didn't have assigned work stations in our class and everyone shared equipment. after that i started using hand sanitizer regularly for the first time in my life*.

anyway, krista texted me tonight and asked if i wanted to hangout and gave me an address. it

---

* ok honestly this is something i should have started doing a long time ago. just from using public bathrooms i know that ~80% of dudes don't wash their hands so anytime you touch anything in public there's a very high chance that same thing was touched by one of those guys. in work bathrooms [cont.]

turned out to be julia's house where her and emily and brandon were hanging out. it turns out emily has a small/medium black pit bull mix w the widest face i've ever seen. i said "wow her face looks like a naked semi truck" and i'm not sure what i meant exactly but it seems accurate. she was wearing a small sweater that had a skull and crossbones crocheted into it. when i got home i posted a new life event on fb that said "pet a dog in a small sweater" that got ~80 likes.

---

it's a smaller percentage, probably guys feel pressured to wash their hands when they know they'll have to see the other people in the bathroom every day. it's probably more around ~40% but still that's way higher than i'm comfortable with. i definitely recommend people get more into using hand santizer, but also dudes if you're reading this pls start washing your hands more thanks.

10.17 ~ ~ full

audrey and i met on tinder and hung out a few times but haven't seen each other in awhile. we follow each other on instagram and i saw that she just adopted a small white dog with orange markings and so i asked if she wanted to grab coffee. when i knocked on her door there was a single sad bark and she said that was the first time she'd heard pablo bark, who had just gotten fixed and was lying on the couch, awake but exhausted looking. his full name is "pablo aktrite ultralight beam ray" which i guess are some pop culture references i don't get.

10.26 ~ ~ waning crescent

i went to a party at my co-worker denton's place that turned out to just be like a get together for a bunch of ppl from my training class. denton has a medium/large dog named adele who was really freaked out by all the people. everyone else was drunk and ignoring her so i sat on the ground and talked to her and after awhile she started licking my face and then we took a selfie together.

11.5 ~ ~ first quarter

neil is an enigma, he's both the weirdest and the most immediately-likable person i've ever met in my life. he's another one of my new coworkers and his second job is as a personal trainer. on the first day of class he told us about his dog zero who's a white and brown corgi. one night joel got drunk and nicknamed zero 'sir zebokins von butter nubs of wales the third' and "knighted" him with a stale baguette. my other coworker jacob and i talked to him about working out and he said he had full access to the gym he works at even after it closes. we made plans to all go after we got off work sometime but that didn't end up happening until tonight. i was the last one to get there and as soon as i walked in the door zero rushed up to me and jumped around me. i pet him for awhile and when i tried to use any of the machines he'd jump up onto my lap, so it turned into less of a workout and more into me just petting zero and talking to neil about zero.

11.14 ~ ~ full

behind my work is a wash with a walking/biking trail around it so on all of my breaks i go out there to get fresh air and hear birds and decompress from talking to verizon's terrible customers. tonight when i was walking back from the trail i heard neil talking to someone (neil has a very distinct voice, if you've ever seen the chocolate rain video then you already know more or less exactly how he sounds). it was dark out but when i got close enough to the smoking section i saw a small white dog sniffing around and trying to eat rocks on the ground. the person neil was talking to turned out to be the dog's owner. she told me the dog is 10 months old and named winter. he's an emotional support dog so she's allowed to bring him to work with her. she picked him up while we were talking and she continued to smoke and it kept getting blown into winter's face. i wanted to say "what the fuck are you doing? are you literally trying to kill your dog?" but i'm too socially awkward to be confrontational and i was upset with myself for not being able to say anything about it so i just went back inside.

11.17 ~ ~ waning gibbous

nicole and i met on tinder back in july but only talked for a few days and then not at all until a few days ago when she texted me and said we should hang out soon. we met for coffee last night at like 8 then walked around downtown for a long time talking and then went back to my apartment and watched beginners (my fav sad movie highly recommend). today we drove up towards the top of mt. lemmon and we stopped a little over half way up and she set up a hammock between 2 birch trees. we read and ate snacks and napped. after awhile i asked if i could meet the dog that was in all of her tinder pics and she said yeah so we packed everything up and drove back down.

nicole lived in a subdivision in the foothills of mt. lemmon that her dad and his business partner's company had built years ago. the only reason she was living there was bc the foundation was falling apart and a lot of other zoning nightmares so the house couldn't be sold or rented and so she got to live there for free until those things got fixed. the house itself was like a mini-mansion and was by far the biggest and nicest house i've ever been in. nicole said she was embarrassed to bring ppl there bc of how empty it was except for the small corner of it her stuff occupied. when we walked in the door val came running up. she's a small black and white—umm, i actually don't know what breed she is, she's one of those dogs with bulging eyes but i think she was probably mixed with something else too. usually in the process of writing this book i'll text the people in it i know if i have a question about their dog, but almost immediately after this day nicole ghosted me and i deleted her number bc i was lonely and had really enjoyed hanging out with her and was worried at some point i'd end up texting her again and i didn't want to annoy her.

11.24 ~ ~ waning crescent

audrey and i started talking again about a week ago and we talked enthusiastically about making a big vegan thanksgiving meal but i didn't think it would actually happen. then yesterday she texted me and we made plans to make a vague "vegan feast".

today steve and i went over to her house and when we walked in pablo started barking and acting "not very right" and there was another dog in her house that was slightly smaller than medium sized and looked majestic af. it turned out it's her ex's dog frida—they have this deal where she watches his dog when he's out of town and vice versa. steve and i had brought a bunch of random food from our place but we still weren't sure what we were going to make. we brainstormed and audrey wrote ideas on her white board and then i drove us all to the grocery store.

we tried going to whole foods first but they were closed, so we went to fry's and when we walked in there was a man who seemed upset we were there and said they were closing in 10 minutes. we found everything we needed and were out in under 5.

we made vegan mac and cheese, stuffing, tofurkey, and baked brussels sprouts and potatoes and other veggies. audrey's kitchen is tiny so we each took turns doing some of the work as the other 2 people played with the dogs.

12.1 ~ ~ waxing crescent

steve and i were hanging out on the couch when we heard a knock at the door. we turned around to look out the window and saw 2 cops outside. steve opened the door and one of the officers asked if we know the guy whose apartment shares the back wall of our apartment. we've never met him and the officer told us the man had been making direct threats about hurting himself and that they thought he might have a gun. the cop said they were going to try to go in and talk to him and asked if we had someplace else we could be for a while. "in case things go wrong, you know, thin walls." steve said, "yeah we were actually just talking about going over to the cemetery to watch the sunset*, so we could go do that." the second cop had been looking off to the side the entire time but now was looking at us like we'd asked to borrow his squad car. "ok yeah," the first cop said. "maybe you should go do that."

steve and i left the apartment and walked the long

---

* this actually wasn't a weird thing for us to do, steve and i watched the sunset together every day whenever we were both home and we usually went to the huge cemetery across the street bc it had the best view of the sky than any other place we'd found within walking distance from our apartment.

way around to get to the other side of our apartment complex so we didn't have to pass by our back neighbor's apartment. we saw more cops walking around and when we turned a corner we saw a bunch of our neighbors hanging out on a patch of grass. there was a man with a dog and i asked him if i could pet his dog and he said yeah. he asked if we got kicked out of our apartment too. the dog was named ziggy and he was a scraggly medium sized doodle mix. when steve and i walked away the man called after us, "stay safe."

12.6 ~ ~ first quarter

i was running late for work and when i was trying to find a spot in the parking lot i saw my coworker alex walking a huge gigantic and mostly dirty-white/gray dog with black markings. when i went inside i told the people who were left in my training class (we started with 19 and by now there were only 5 of us, everyone else having quit at various points during the 12 week training course) and we all went outside to pet the dog. alex's partner had brought the dog here to surprise alex on his break. i was so excited about the dog that i didn't clock in until i was ~15 minutes late.

12.8 ~ ~ waxing gibbous

i met up with nirantha at a coffee house. we have a bunch of mutual friends and have been talking to each other for a long time online and through texts about how we should hang out and today we finally did. she told me about how she went to los angeles the other day for a job interview with nasa and had a skype interview with apple a few days later. the chair i was sitting on faced the patio where i could see a yellow lab looking in thru the glass door. i said i wished the dog knew how to open doors so it could come in, then i told nirantha about the list of dogs i pet that i was hoping to eventually turn into a book. a little later she pointed out the window towards a woman who was carrying a small dog in her arms and said "look at that dog." the woman walked into the coffee house and came up to our table and it turned out to be someone nirathna knew from when she lived in denver. the dog was a 10 week old pup named ken and i got to pet him while nirantha and the woman talked for a little bit. after she walked away nirantha asked me if ken was going to be in my book now and i nodded and said "ken is definitely gonna be in the book." a little later someone opened the patio door for the golden retriever and it walked around sniffing under each table and when it went under our table we both pet it while continuing our conversation like nothing was happening.

12.16 ~ ~ **waning gibbous**

guess where me and cori met lol yea it was tinder. anyway she wanted to take me to this thing called winter haven that's just this huge, middleclass-y neighborhood that goes way over the top on christmas decorations every year. there's no traffic allowed through and it seems super inconvenient for the ppl who live there but they decide to do it anyway. it's a big and well known thing in tucson and it seems mainly for families and kids. the only part of it i really enjoyed was there were so many dogs there but being around that many people felt draining and awkward and i didn't feel confident enough to ask anyone if i could pet their dog. deep in the heart of the neighborhood was a house with a water fountain display that was synchronized with music. cori and i were watching it when she pointed in front of us at a small white puffy dog in a santa style sweater. cori said, "mrs. claus." i walked up to the doggo and she smelled my fingers and then licked them a little bit and i think we would have spent more time together but she walked away bc the person holding the other end of her leash started to walk away.

12.18 ~ ~ waning gibbous

ok so remember that wash behind my work? well it's extremely long and winds itself thru mostly all of northern tucson. there's a walking path that goes along it and every day on my hour-long lunch break i walk off in one direction and see how far i can get before having to turn back. today on my way back i came across an old man walking 3 dogs. 1 was as very close to me as she could go on her leash and staring intently at me and seemed v excited i was coming closer. when i got up to her i asked the man if i could pet his dog and he made some guttural noises that sounded affirmative so i held out my hand for pupper to smell and lick and then one of the others came up and pushed that one out of the way and let me pet him. i asked the man what the dog's names are and he said the first one i pet was foxy, the other cotton, and the third i don't remember but it was something like brown sugar or some type of seasoning. i stood up to keep walking and then brown sugar came up to me so i bent down to pet her and said "hi brown sugar you're the smallest and i love you" and the old man laughed.

12.23 ~ ~ waning crescent

my aunt and uncle drove down from prescott valley to visit me for the day. i don't think i've seen either of them since angela's wedding ~14 months ago. they brought their small fluffy dog lucy who's now a lot older and less fluffy than i remember her. we sat in my apartment talking and when they asked what i've been up to they were surprised to hear i'd wrote a book. i gave them a copy and then felt weird bc they've never seen that side of me and i said "i should probably warn you, it's kind of sad." we drove to a mediterranean restaurant that i don't think was actually a mediterranean restaurant, i'm not sure what it was but my uncle kept calling it a mediterranean restaurant. the only thing on the menu that was vegan was an entrée that turned out to be just a big plate of baked eggplant slices. my uncle told me stories about his family's history and it was really interesting and i kept wondering how he could remember so many details about things that had happened so long ago, then i wondered if that was something that comes naturally for most people and it only seemed impressive to me bc my memory and speaking skills are maybe less developed than most people.

when we got back into the car lucy was asleep and

my aunt woke her up to feed her some food she'd saved in a napkin. on the way back they wanted to stop at a vegan bakery and even though i don't like sweets i still appreciated the sentiment, it was a good mix of their interests and mine. they bought some snacks for their drive home and then dropped me back off at my apartmnet. they told me i should come visit sometime and that i could stay in their guest bedroom and i told them that sounded really nice.

12.27 ~ ~ new

i came into work and decided today's my last day. they call this position 'customer service representative' but really we're only here so customers have somebody to yell at. we're practically incentivized to not give good customer service. every time we issue a credit back to a customer it counts against our stats. every time we transfer a call to another department it counts against our stats. ok two examples is enough. our stats determine our monthly bonus, so they're important to us. we get paid a wage that's below the poverty line and our employer says that's fine bc "if you do your job well" we'll get a good bonus. so if you get a good bonus that means you have good stats, and if you have good stats it means you gave customers poor service—basically you didn't do everything you could to help the customers you talked to. this job has taught me that what companies mean by "customer service representatives" is "employees who service the customer in a way that's most beneficial to the company".

ok just 2 more things and we'll get to today's dog i promise it's a good one. the parts of our stats that are weighted most heavily are 'disconnects' and 'surveys'. the goal for disconnects (aka people canceling their service) is to only have one per 100 calls you take. the process for it is lengthly and almost always pisses the customer off. we have to offer them "save the line" options which are like discounts and things the customer can take advantage of if they keep the line (these offers are typically nothing special and usually just mentioning things they could do with the line in general, like switching to prepay). after you've exhausted all the options the system gives, you have to put the customer on hold and find a supervisor (and supervisors don't want to help you bc approving disconnects counts against their stats too. i had a call once where someone wanted to disconnect all 5 of their family's lines bc they switched providers and when i went to my direct supervisor he got angrier than i'd ever seen him before and he refused to do it and told me to just "figure it out"). the sup asks what you've offered and then tells you other things to offer, so you have to get back on the phone and offer the customer other options that they don't want and this whole time the customer is getting more and more pissed bc they already made up their mind before calling and all they want is for you to stop wasting their time and just disconnect their service and to not be harassed for 10 minutes about it.

the second thing is surveys, which are calls customers receive from an automated system ~10 minutes after they get off the phone with a rep. this call asks them if they are satisfied with verizon after the service they received. there's only a yes/no answer with no gray area in between. the goal for survey's is 93% which means for ever 15 surveys you get you can only get a "no" on one. surveys are weighted toward our bonus the most heavily and here's why: if you do everything the way you were trained to and service customers in the best interest of the company then your stats are probably going to be pretty good, which would mean you'd expect to get a good bonus on next month's check. but only considering the company's interests is going to make customers upset, so they'll fail all of your surveys which tanks your bonus.

and yea sure there's another side to that, if you only focus on making customers happy and not worrying about having good stats besides for surveys that could potential get you a nice bonus each month. but if the rest of your stats are consistently low enough then you get let go, so [in the original manuscript i had that one shrug emoticon inserted here but for whatever reason the characters won't paste into indesign so like just imagine that's here instead of this explanation].

ok /end rant woo all right so i'm halfway thru my last day which means it's lunchtime and i'm out walking on the trail next to the wash. it's busier today than usual. i see a group of ~7 ppl farther down the trail that are walking the same direction as i am. i assume it's a family (mom, dad, several smaller children and teenagers). if i haven't mentioned this before i have extreme social anxiety and for some reason the thought of having to walk past these people fills me with high amounts of stress. i think about just slowing down or even just sitting on a nearby bench and spending the rest of my break there, but i know this will probably be the last time i ever walk on this trail and i want to go further on it than i ever have before. i start walking a lot faster so i can spend as little time near them as possible (and so hopefully they won't try starting a conversation). when i get closer i see they're walking a really beautiful australian shepherd and i think about how i want to pet it so i can put today in the dog book i'm hopefully going to someday write, so i can talk about how this is my last day of work and vent about the hypocrisies of my job.

i pass the family by walking as far on the other side of the path as i can from them and when i'm across from the dog he looks up at me and starts walking over by my. "he wants your peanut butter sandwich" the group's dad says to me about the peanut butter sandwich i'm eating while i walk. i think it's weird the dad can tell it's a peanut butter sandwich from how far i am from them but i slow down and walk just close enough so i can pet the dog and i say "hi doggo." the dad says "his name's sydney" and then laughs and i do a little fake laugh that sounds like a little real laugh and the dad says "because he's an australian shepherd. like the city." i tell him my mom has an australian shepherd/poodle mix and he asks me what i said and i give him a little wave and say "have a nice day," then i start walking fast again.

12.31 ~ ~ waxing crescent

well this has been 2016. i quit the job i had been at for 3 years and moved to the other side of the country into a house full of strangers i met on the internet. from there i went on to share an apartment with the person whose poetry had first inspired me to start writing poetry a year and a half ago. i found a new job and published my first book. four days ago i quit that job and 2 days ago i found a new job working at another—but, supposedly, less stressful—call center. things changed a lot for me this year, but no matter what happened or where i went, there were always dogs to pet, always the same 8 phases of the moon to look up at.

jonathan and i got ramen tonight at a small japanese restaurant that was across the street from the phó place we'd originally tried to go but was closed. it was out first time hanging out since newport beach and it was really nice to catch up. he told me he'd recently adopted a pit bull pup named boots from a shelter and then literally the next day one of his employees brought in a pit bull/ bulldog puppy that he'd found hanging out in the street on his way into work. jonathan ended up adopting her too and named her charlie. he told me i should come over and meet them sometime and i said, "what about after this?" we were both going to nirantha's new years eve party later so we decided we'd go hangout at his house until it started and then leave from there. when we went into his house both of the puppies started jumping up on me and i sat down on the couch with my arm around them on either side of me as they kept jumping up to lick my face while simultaneously trying to push the other one out of the way. i was almost in tears from how much love they had to give and i just kept saying, "this is the best day of my life."

the earth is over 4 billion years old and 99% of
the species that have ever lived here are now
extinct and i'm just really thankful to be alive in
this small sliver of time where humans and dogs
coexist together.

joseph parker okay lives in tucson, az. he's the author of *every time i park my car i feel like i'm doing something wrong* (a winner of nostrovia press's 2017 chapbook contest) and *my phone is about to die and i hope it takes me with it*. He's the founder of the literary journal spy kids review and the publishing house 2fast2house. more of his work can be found at gumroad.com/josephparkerokay. he tweets @verysoftlake.

www.ingramcontent.com/pod-product-compliance
Lightning Source LLC
Chambersburg PA
CBHW070316120726
47910CB00007B/2505